For Mike and Amy

Library of Congress Cataloging-in-Publication Data

Northway, Jennifer, 1955–
Get lost, Laura! / Jennifer Northway.
p.   cm.
"Artists & Writers Guild Books."
Summary: When cousins Lucy and Alice find that Lucy's little sister Laura keeps
pestering them, the older girls decide to play hide-and-seek to avoid Laura.
[1. Sisters–Fiction. 2. Cousins–Fiction. 3. Hide-and-seek–Fiction.
4. Responsibility–Fiction. 5. Blacks–England–Fiction.] I. Title.
PZ7.N8195Ge 1995   [E]–dc20   94-22257   CIP   AC

First published in Great Britain in 1993 by Scholastic Publications Ltd.

Get Lost, Laura!

JENNIFER NORTHWAY

ARTISTS & WRITERS GUILD BOOKS

Golden Books

Western Publishing Company, Inc.

Lucy and her cousin Alice were playing dress-up.
"Let's pretend we're going to a ball," said Lucy.
"I'm in the carriage already," said Alice,
swinging on the garden gate. "Quick, get in!"

As Lucy wobbled to the gate in her mother's
high-heeled shoes, Laura grabbed one of them.
"I want them!" she said.

"Let go, Laura," said Lucy angrily, but she did give the shoes to her little sister. Then she put on a green pair. Laura wanted those, too.

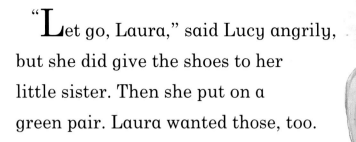

"How many feet do you think you've got?" sighed Lucy, handing them over. "Why don't you go and play in the sandbox."
But Laura reached for Lucy's big hat and grabbed the cherries. They broke off and rolled away like marbles into the vegetable garden.
"*Get lost*, Laura!" said Lucy. "*Go away!*"

But Laura didn't go away. She stuck the big hat on her head.

"I'm mad at Laura," Lucy hissed to Alice. "Let's hide."

"But your mom says we have to play with her," whispered Alice.

"We can still keep an eye on her," said Lucy as she tiptoed toward the end of the garden. "Let's play hide-and-seek, Laura! You're *it*!"

9

Alice pulled open the shed door.

"Quick, let's hide," she said.

"Dad doesn't let us come in here," said Lucy. "He says it's not safe."

"We'll be very careful," said Alice.

The shed smelled of paint and mildew, and was full of tools and flowerpots. They found an old baby carriage, but they couldn't get it out from behind the junk.

"Look," said Lucy, "there's a big hole in the planks here. Maybe it's a secret passage." They squeezed through and found themselves in the garden next door. Lucy's neighbor was sitting in a deck chair reading the paper.

"Is that two cats I see in my flower bed?" she asked. "Your daddy needs to fix that hole, Lucy, otherwise *I* might crawl through and give *you* a scare!" But the neighbor was smiling. Lucy and Alice wriggled back into the shed. Alice's dress caught on a plank and ripped all the way down one side.

13

"I'm glad I don't have a baby sister," said Alice. "Babies are yucky. They're always wet and they dribble."

"Laura's all right," said Lucy. "She's dribbling because she's still getting her teeth. Mom will be angry if she sees we're not playing with her." She opened the shed door.

"Come and find us, Laura!" she called.

There was silence.

"I wonder where she's gone," said Alice. They looked all around the shed, and then under it, but there was no sign of Laura.

There weren't many other places to look.

Alice pulled all the clothes out of the suitcase.

Lucy looked in the vegetable garden. They were full of scrunchy snails and slimy slugs, but Laura wasn't under them.

Alice lifted the garbage can lid and peered in, but shut it quickly —
even Laura wouldn't hide in *there*.

"She couldn't have gone far," said Alice. "Her legs are too little."

"She can move really fast when she wants to," said Lucy.
"Look, Alice! You left the gate open after you were swinging on it!"

There were some boys playing football in the field beyond the gate,
but there was no sign of Laura.

Lucy called over the wall to her other neighbor, Julie.

"Have you seen Laura anywhere?" she asked.

"You didn't leave the gate open, did you?" said Julie.
"You'd better go and tell your mother while I check the
playing field." And she hurried off.

"Do you think she's really lost?" said Alice. "Monsters or anything might get her."

"I don't believe in monsters," said Lucy bravely. "Maybe she crawled into the shed when we came out, and she wants us to find her."

But she wasn't in the shed. So they wriggled
through the hole again into the flower bed
next door, but she wasn't there either.

Lucy began to panic. As they rushed back
through the shed, Lucy knocked over
a jar of black paint.

"I wish we'd never come in here!" Lucy shouted angrily. "I *said* we shouldn't! It's all *your* fault, Alice!"

"*You're* the one who wanted to hide!" said Alice.

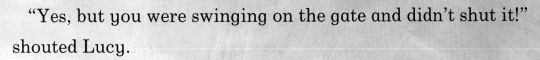

"Yes, but you were swinging on the gate and didn't shut it!" shouted Lucy.

"She's *your* sister, and *you* shouldn't have left her!" Alice shouted back. "*I* said we shouldn't. I bet you get in trouble!"

Lucy burst into tears. "Mom'll be furious," she wailed. "I'll have to run away, too!" Then Alice began to feel sorry.

"Don't do that," Alice said. "That'll mean two children lost instead of one. Anyway, it *was* partly my fault. I hope they don't say we can never play together again." And she started to cry, too.

"I'd better tell Mom," sniffed Lucy. "I wish I'd never told Laura to get lost." She pushed open the kitchen door *very* slowly . . . and there, sitting on her mother's lap, was Laura!

"Laura!" cried Alice. "You were here all the time!"

"Don't get mad, Mom," said Lucy, wiping her eyes on her mother's sleeve. "I know we should have been watching her. We looked for her *everywhere*! We're so sorry."

Laura slid off her mother's lap. She liked the look of Lucy's fancy barrette and tried to pull it out of her hair.

"Ow!" said Lucy. "Get . . ."
She *was* going to say, "Get lost, Laura!"

. . . but she didn't!